211

W9-CTH-931

Valentine's Day

Dorothy Goeller

Bailey Books
an imprint of
Enslow Publishers, Inc.
40 Industrial Road
Box 398
Berkeley Heights, NJ 07922
USA

http://www.enslow.com

Bailey Books, an imprint of Enslow Publishers, Inc.

Copyright © 2011 by Enslow Publishers, Inc.

All rights reserved.

No part of this book may be reproduced by any means without the written permission of the publisher.

Library of Congress Cataloging-in-Publication Data

Goeller, Dorothy.
  Valentine's day / Dorothy Goeller.
       p. cm. — (All about holidays)
  Includes index.
  Summary: "Simple text and photographs present a story with a Valentine's Day theme"—Provided by publisher.
  ISBN 978-0-7660-3810-3
  1. Valentine's Day—Juvenile literature. I. Title.
  GT4925.G64 2011
  394.2618—dc22   2010012570
Paperback ISBN: 978-1-59845-178-8

Printed in the United States of America

062010 Lake Book Manufacturing, Inc., Melrose Park, IL

10 9 8 7 6 5 4 3 2 1

To Our Readers: We have done our best to make sure all Internet Addresses in this book were active and appropriate when we went to press. However, the author and the publisher have no control over and assume no liability for the material available on those Internet sites or on other Web sites they may link to. Any comments or suggestions can be sent by e-mail to comments@enslow.com or to the address on the back cover.

♻ Enslow Publishers, Inc., is committed to printing our books on recycled paper. The paper in every book contains 10% to 30% post-consumer waste (PCW). The cover board on the outside of each book contains 100% PCW. Our goal is to do our part to help young people and the environment too!

Photo Credits: Shutterstock.com

Cover Photo: © 2010 Photos.com, a division of Getty Images. All rights reserved

Note to Parents and Teachers

Help pre-readers get a jumpstart on reading. These lively stories introduce simple concepts with repetition of words and short simple sentences. Photos and illustrations fill the pages with color and effectively enhance the text. Free Educator Guides are available for this series at www.enslow.com. Search for the *All About Holidays* series name.

Contents

Words to Know

heart   hearts

How many hearts?

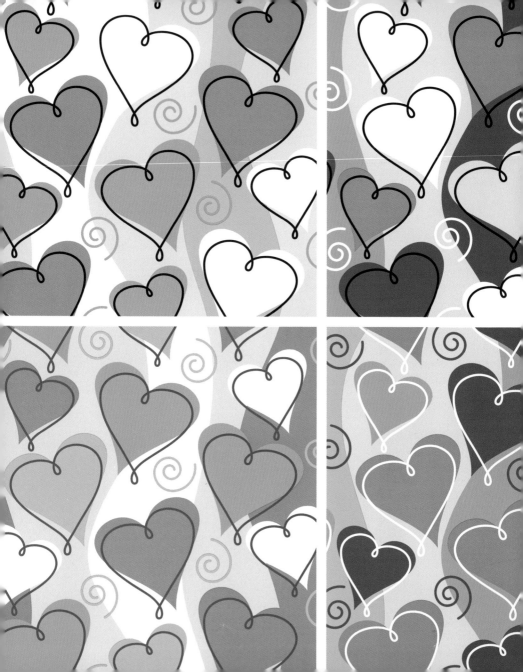

Too many!

How many hearts?

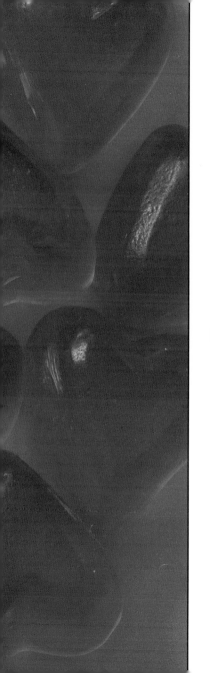

Too many!

How many hearts?

Too many!

How many hearts?

17

Too many!

TOO MANY!

One heart is best!

Read More

Holub, Joan. *Big Heart!: A Valentine's Day Story.* New York: Aladdin, 2007.

Rylant, Cynthia. *If You'll Be My Valentine.* New York: HarperCollins, 2005.

Web Sites

DLTK's Valentine's Day Activities for Kids. <http://dltk-holidays.com/valentines/index.htm>

Kaboose.com:Valentine's Day 2010: Valentine' Day Ideas. <http://holidays.kaboose.com/valentines-day/>

Index

Guided Reading Level: **B**
Guided Reading Leveling System is based on the guidelines recommended by Fountas and Pinnell.

Word Count: 26